Barbie™
of
Swan Lake

A Panorama Sticker Storybook

Written by Jill L. Goldowsky

Photography by Willy Lew, Laura Lynch, Lars Auvinen, Johannes Auvinen, Greg Roccia, Michael Corona, Susan Cracraft, Vicki Tran, Lisa Bellow, Meghen Sepanik, Jason Tsuno, Judy Tsuno, and Lisa Collins

Reader's Digest
Children's Books™

Pleasantville, New York • Montréal, Québec • Bath, United Kingdom

Long ago, a beautiful girl named Odette lived in a small village with her family. Everyone loved Odette. She was sweet, happy, and kind.

Odette's family owned a bakery. Every day, she helped her father bake mouthwatering pies and delicious breads. Odette's sister Marie helped, too, but she was often out racing

her horse through town or attending village dances. Odette wasn't daring like her sister. She preferred to be with her father in the bakery. She never thought of herself as brave. Little did she know, she was.

On the other side of the village, atop a small hill, lived the queen and her son, Prince Daniel. The prince was a handsome and fun-loving young man. He was a very talented archer and often impressed people with what he could do with his bow and arrow. He never missed a target, no matter how difficult the shot.

The queen was proud of her son, but she thought he was filled with too many dreams of great adventures. She wanted him to settle down and get married. She was planning a royal ball for all the princesses in the land to attend so that he could pick a bride.

Back in the village, a unicorn came dashing down the street. Odette had never seen such a sight! The villagers tried capturing the creature with a rope, but the unicorn escaped from their grasp. As it ran toward the forest for safety, part of the rope dangled dangerously from its neck. Odette followed the unicorn into the woods—she wanted to keep it from harm. But once inside the forest, the rope caught onto a branch. Odette quickly spotted a crystal with a sharp edge wedged inside a tree. She yanked it out and cut the unicorn free.

Just then, a beautiful Fairy Queen, surrounded by magical animals, appeared. "You're going to save us and our home," she said.

"I don't understand," said Odette.

"My evil cousin Rothbart is taking over the forest with his magic powers," explained the Fairy Queen. "But it is said that the one who frees the Magic Crystal will overcome Rothbart and save the forest."

"You have the wrong girl," said Odette. "I'm not brave enough to save a forest."

As Lila the unicorn was showing Odette the way out of the Enchanted Forest, Rothbart suddenly appeared in front of them.

"So, you freed the Magic Crystal," Rothbart sneered at Odette. He raised his hand to reveal a ring—the source of his powerful magic. Then, a frightening bolt flashed forth and circled Odette in a spinning cloud. Terrified, Odette looked down at herself. Rothbart had turned her into a swan!

The Fairy Queen rushed to Odette's side and placed a tiara with the Magic Crystal in it on Odette's head.

"As long as you have the Magic Crystal, Rothbart can't harm you," she explained. "I can turn you back into your human form from sunset to dawn, like I've done for the elves," she said. "But during the day you will be a swan, until the spell is broken. You need to find the Book of Forest Lore to break the secret of Rothbart's spell on your own."

Lila and Odette traveled through the forest to the Magic Vault to find the Book of Forest Lore. The book was guarded by a friendly troll named Erasmus.

Lila, Odette, and Erasmus searched for the Book of Forest Lore inside the Magic Vault all night, but never found it. Soon daybreak came and Rothbart's evil spell turned Odette back into a swan once more. Although Odette was determined to find the book, she headed back to the lake empty-handed.

Meanwhile, Rothbart had magically lured Prince Daniel into the Enchanted Forest, hoping he'd shoot Odette in swan form with his bow and arrow. Sensing danger, Odette quickly flew into the air. She landed just as the sun set, turning back into her human form.

"Who are you?" asked the prince, greatly taken with her beauty.

Odette was surprised to see the prince standing before her. As she told him her story, their friendship bloomed. Little did they know that Rothbart was watching them!

Rothbart suddenly appeared in front of them, angry that his plot had not worked. "One arrow from a human would've killed her!" Rothbart raged. He raised his hand to punish the prince with a powerful bolt of magic. But Odette jumped in front of him to repel the bolt with the Magic Crystal, saving the prince from Rothbart!

Odette and Prince Daniel spent the rest of the night in the Enchanted Forest, surrounded by elves and fairies. He asked Odette to attend the ball the following evening. When the sun began to rise, he returned to the castle.

Later that day, Erasmus brought good news to Odette and her friends—he had found the Book of Forest Lore and the way to break Rothbart's spell! It read: *The one who frees the Magic Crystal will share a love so true it will overcome all evil magic. But if the true love pledges love to another, the Magic Crystal will lose its power.*

As Erasmus explained the secret to his friends, Rothbart kidnapped him to get the book. Rothbart devised a plan. His daughter Odile would go to the ball and his magic would make Prince Daniel think that Odile was really Odette! Once the prince declared his love to the wrong girl, the power of the Magic Crystal would be broken!

Rothbart and Odile arrived at the castle just before sunset. The prince was delighted to see the girl he thought he had met the night before. He took her onto the dance floor and danced with his new love.

Outside, Odette was flying as fast as she could to reach the castle. She and the elves had rescued Erasmus from Rothbart's evil palace and learned of Rothbart's plan to trick the prince.

Odette arrived in time to hear the prince ask Odile to marry him. The magic of the crystal was gone and Odette fell to the ground.

Realizing now that Rothbart had tricked him, the prince went after the evil wizard.

Rothbart grabbed the Magic Crystal from Odette's tiara and put it around his neck. The prince attacked, but Rothbart shot a bolt of evil magic from his ring in defense. Odette and Prince Daniel tried to save each other, but the power of the crystal was gone.

Rothbart rejoiced over his victory—and then something amazing happened. The power of true love lit the crystal once more, and Rothbart disappeared in a shower of sparks.

Prince Daniel and Odette awoke to find everyone from the forest transformed back to their natural forms. Rothbart and his evil magic were gone forever! That evening, Odette was reunited with her father during a celebration honoring Odette and Prince Daniel.

"You've been so brave," said her father. "Now you're going to marry a prince. I'm so proud of you."

That night, the most magical thing in the forest was Odette's and Prince Daniel's love.